THE JERSEY VIGNETTES

A RUSSIAN GUNS NOVELLA

BETHANY-KRIS

Published by Bethany-Kris

www.bethanykris.com

ISBN 13: 978-1-988197-07-4
eISBN 13: 978-1-988197-06-7

For the fans of this series. I know you didn't want it to end, and that you wanted to see this family continue on forever. I did, too. I will forever miss this family, but thank for loving them like you did.

CONTENTS

CHAPTER ONE

"Ana …"

"Mmm, yes?"

"Look at me," Koldan demanded.

"Nope."

Ana rolled over in the bed, burying her face into the pillow. It smelled like Koldan's woodsy scent and Ana's sugared lotions. She thought that mixing the two scents together had to be one of the very best things she'd ever smelled in her life.

Then again, she was biased.

"*Ana.*"

"It should be illegal for you to wake me up this early," Ana grumbled.

"But it isn't, so look at me," Koldan murmured.

Ana sighed, feeling the strong hands of her lover ghost over her naked skin under the soft sheets. His touches were relentless in their intent, determined to wake her up for whatever nonsense he had planned. Ana was beginning to think she might like his nonsense if he kept touching her like he was.

"I'm up," Ana said as Koldan kissed her shoulder blade.

"Are you?"

"Very."

"Good." Koldan's hand caught Ana's under the blanket. "We have things to do today and I want to get an early start."

"Like what?" Ana asked.

"Things," he repeated.

"Koldan."

"But I think we'll start with this."

Ana felt something slide down her finger under the blanket. The weight of the jewelry surprised her. Slowly, Ana pulled her hand out from under the sheet to see the pearl and diamond engagement ring adorning her hand. It sparkled under the early morning light filtering into the bedroom window of her apartment.

"Oh, my God," Ana whispered.

"We can start from there," Koldan said, chuckling.

"That's … beautiful."

"I thought so."

"I love pearls," Ana said.

Koldan grinned, nodding. "So your father informed me."

Well, that was a little surprising. Sometimes Koldan and her father didn't see eye to eye where Ana was concerned.

"You talked to Anton?"

"Yes, and he threatened to kill me along with a few other … *things*."

Ana laughed, feeling high spun. "I don't know what to say."

"I thought of a million and one different ways to ask you. Nothing really worked for you or I. Flashier ways, bigger ways—"

"Don't," Ana interjected firmly, giving Koldan a look that shut him up.

"Okay."

"This is perfect."

"Is it?" he asked softly.

"Us, quiet love, early morning sunlight, and a bed. What's not to love?"

"Perfect," he echoed.

Ana pulled him closer to her. "My answer is yes."

Koldan smirked. "I thought it would be."

CHAPTER TWO

Two years later …

"Ana, I'm dying here," Koldan said quietly.

Ana Avdonin hid her grin from her fiancé, knowing if he saw, Koldan would find the truth in her teasing. There was no denying the fact that Ana could be a little difficult. She was particular, sometimes hard to please, and she didn't deny any of it for a second. Koldan Vasin was the second man in her life who managed to make Ana happy.

The first was her father.

Anton Avdonin, Bratva mob boss and arms trafficker, had raised Ana with the belief that if—not when—she ever found a man to stand by her side in life, that man should be worthy of the position. Because to Anton, Ana was his little Queen.

That meant only a proper King was fit for her.

"Ana," Koldan said again.

She could hear him shift on his feet behind her like he was uncomfortable.

"Yes?"

"*Krasivyy*, we've walked through the whole damn house."

His pet name made her smile grow. He'd always called her beautiful even at her ugliest; even in her worst moments, she was goddamn beautiful to him.

Koldan was worthy.

Ana loved him all the more for it.

"The colors turned out great," Ana said, reaching out to let her fingers trail over the painted walls.

"I hoped you would say that," Koldan replied, his relief loud and clear.

Ana finally turned to face him, allowing him to see her grin. "I know I was difficult about the house sometimes."

"Difficult, Ana?"

"What would you call it?" Ana asked.

Koldan opened his mouth to say something, but shut it just as fast. "Perfect, babe. You were great. And it looks great."

"It does."

The house Koldan had built for them was amazing. Three floors plus a basement.

It was a six bedroom, five-and-a-half bath paradise. From the color schemes to the Italian marble in the kitchen and the tiles in their master bath ordered in from India, Ana had her hand in a little bit of everything. Koldan stepped back, gave her the check book, and let her do what she wanted.

Our house, he'd said. *Make it ours.*

"I wanted everything to be perfect," Ana said, shrugging.

"It is," Koldan said. Then, he eyed her curiously. "It is, right?"

"I'm glad all the furniture came in before the wedding," Ana replied instead.

Koldan sighed. "What's wrong with the house, Ana?"

Ana grinned widely. "Nothing."

"Nothing?"

"Nada."

Koldan shook his head, laughing under his breath. "You put me through hell for the last hour and a half while I wondered what was going on in your head and all this time, you loved it?"

"Yep."

"Nasty girl," her fiancé muttered.

Ana winked. "I have to get my kicks somehow, Koldan. You're an easy target."

"Only to you."

"Exactly."

Ana waved at the room they stood in.

The bedroom was directly across from their master bedroom. The walls were white instead of a pale cream like she'd asked for.

"Is this the only thing that's left to be finished?"

Koldan smiled. "No. It is finished."

Ana raised a single brow. "No, it isn't. I know what color these walls were supposed to be."

It was also the only room in the house missing its furniture, if Ana considered it.

"And where is the bedroom set and the leather seating for here?" Ana asked.

Koldan cleared his throat. "I canceled the orders for this room."

Ana's confusion jumped sky high. "Why?"

"Because you designed this room over two years ago before the house even had foundation poured, Ana."

"So? Designing is what I do, Koldan. That's why I went to school, remember?" Ana tried not to be angry, but she kind of was. "If you didn't like what I was going to do in here, why didn't you just say something to me about it?"

"I did like it," Koldan replied, unfazed.

"Then why—"

"I think this room might serve a better purpose than being designed and readied for a guest, Ana."

"Like what?" she asked, frustrated.

"Like … a nursery."

Ana froze in place. "Oh."

"It's in the best spot, right across from us. It's big enough. And—"

"Stop," Ana said.

Koldan did, shoving his hands in his pockets. "I wanted to surprise you."

"And apparently you want to have a baby," Ana said.

Koldan chuckled. "Eventually. I just don't see the point in doing this room up for us to only rip it apart and start over someday. Who knows when that day is going to come?"

"The walls could still be painted with a cream color of some sort," Ana mused, her mind taking in the space all over again with new eyes. "Especially if we ever had a girl. I am not doing those ugly pastel colors."

Koldan laughed darky. "So, you're not really all that mad, right?"

No, she wasn't.

Koldan was right, in a way. Ana had designed their home through eyes that had been considering the then and there.

She hadn't considered five or even ten years down the road when they had a family of their own because at the time, starting a family of her own had not been the most important thing on her list.

Hell, it probably hadn't been in the top ten.

"Why didn't you tell me you've been thinking about having children?" Ana asked quietly.

Koldan tipped his head down, hiding his gaze. "I've thought about children with you from the first time I realized I loved you, *krasivyy*."

Oh.

Well, then …

"I can do something else in here," Ana said, willing away the emotion in her tone. "Something nursery themed, I suppose."

Koldan nodded. "Let's do that."

CHAPTER THREE

Little Vera Avdonin had a way about her. There was just something about Ana's niece that drew people in like a moth to the flame. Maybe it was Vera's innocent nature or her bright, open gaze that always seemed to look straight through a person to see what was really on the inside. Ana didn't know for sure what it was about her little niece that put people at ease, but she loved it.

Vera was so different from her father in that way. Demyan, older than Ana by four years, had gone through so much in his life. Sure, Ana suffered through her own things—her sexual assault, the murder of a friend, and the backlash her family received from it all, but Demyan … He was left to raise a little girl all on his own with no one to stand by his side.

Ana never wondered why her brother was so cold, anymore.

"Look," Anton murmured, nodding at Vera.

Vera's hand snuck out and grabbed her father's. A ghost of a smile curved Demyan's mouth as he held his daughter's tiny hand and directed her into line with the other wedding party. He didn't once let her go, not even when the event planner asked him to so that Vera could stand alone in line like she was supposed to.

"He won't let her go until she's ready for him to," Anton said, the hint of amusement playing in his tone. "They remind me a lot of us when you were little, but in a more private way. You made it very clear to anyone who would listen to you that I was your daddy and no one else mattered."

Ana laughed. "You spoiled me."

"Rotten," Anton agreed. "But they are like us. Demyan and Vera, I mean."

Ana never noticed that before, but if she thought back on it hard enough, she knew it was true. Maybe little Vera and Demyan shared the same kind of father and daughter closeness that Ana shared with Anton. With her brother, it was sometimes hard to tell because his walls were so high, no one had the first clue of how to climb over them.

Well, all but two people.

"Claire showed up today," Anton said.

"Did she?" Ana asked.

Anton nodded, smiling. "She's good for them. Demyan is stubborn; Claire is relentless. They're an interesting pair."

"I like her."

"Me, too." Anton chuckled and added, "I give them five months, six at the most."

"Claire and Demyan?"

"Yes."

"Before what?" Ana asked.

"Before I find out we'll be having a second grandbaby to add to the mix."

"Daddy!" Ana scolded. "That's not your business and you know it."

Anton just shrugged like he hadn't said a thing. "Passionate people make waves, Ana. They can't control it. Demyan never was any good at denying things he wanted. I'm not saying it's a bad thing. It's nice to see him woken up again after everything. He deserves someone to make him happy again and for different reasons than why his daughter makes him happy. He should have someone to love."

"It is nice," Ana agreed.

"And I want more grandchildren."

Ana huffed, blowing a curl out of her eye. "Still not your business."

Anton smirked but stayed silent. Ana should have known better. Everything was Anton's business if he wanted it to be, especially where their family was concerned. It was one of the ways he kept them safe from outsiders. Being a Bratva born family and thoroughly immersed in the world of the Russian Mafia, always put a spotlight on them. Anton worked goddamn hard to keep it from shining too brightly.

"And you, too," Anton added like it was an afterthought.

"What about me?" Ana asked.

"I would like some grandchildren from you, *dushka*."

Ana smacked her father's arm, ignoring the curious gazes and laughter that followed from the waiting wedding party. Even Demyan turned to glance over his shoulder at his sister and father with amusement burning behind his usually cold gaze. No one could hear their quiet talk, but still.

"And that's not your business, either," Ana said firmly.

"I'm still annoyed that you're getting married," Anton murmured. "I'm a lot like Demyan in the way I just want to keep holding your hand until you tell me you're ready to let me go. I know you're ready to let go, Ana, but I'm not and that's the hardest thing for me."

"But?"

"But Koldan is a good man, and good men make for good fathers."

Ana smiled, glancing away from her father. "I had a pretty good one, I suppose."

"Damn right, *dushka*."

In her coral colored dress, Vera looked absolutely precious. Demyan, with his usual stony features and stoic stance, screamed at the people near them to stay the hell away. Ana wasn't sure if her brother knew how to be approachable anymore.

Ana felt her father's hand cover hers that was tucked around his arm as they stood side by side behind the wedding party. Her bridesmaids, the maid of honor, and her little flower girl—Vera—waited patiently in line for the progression to start.

Anton patted Ana's hand without saying a word, but she didn't need him to speak. Ana could feel his sadness practically wafting from him. The tender smile didn't leave his face for a second, but Ana knew. Her father was struggling.

It was hard for Ana to see it. The heart attack he'd suffered a couple of months earlier had been enough to scare Ana to the point where she seriously questioned if she could leave New York and her parents behind after the wedding. She didn't want to think about waking up one day to a call that her father had suffered another cardiac arrest.

But, they got through it. Ana's panic lessened and New Jersey was her first stop after her honeymoon to Paris.

"No more tears," Ana told her father.

Anton laughed under his breath and brought her closer to his side. She leaned her head against his broad shoulder, comforted by the position alone. She couldn't count the amount of times in her life where her father had been the only person able to give her a sense of security, total support and unconditional love.

And then Koldan came along, and she added a second person.

Of course, Ana's mother Viviana had been another marking cornerstone in her life, but there had always been a different relationship between Ana and Anton.

"No tears," Anton said quietly. "I love you, Ana."

"I love you, too, Papa."

CHAPTER FOUR

"Ana!"

"Yeah?"

Ana was far too comfortable on the plush chaise that overlooked the windows in her hotel suite to get up and find out what Koldan wanted. Three days into their honeymoon and they had yet to leave the five-star hotel with all its service and beauty. Besides, she had the perfect view of Paris just by looking out her windows. For now, she was content.

No doubt, Koldan would convince her to get up and go outside soon.

"Ana," Koldan said again, popping his head out from the bathroom doorway.

"Yes?"

"Your phone is buzzing with a message," her husband said.

Ana waved it off. "Just check it and let me know what it says."

Koldan made a dismissive sound. "I already did."

She wasn't surprised. Ana didn't really care. She had nothing to hide and neither did Koldan. If she wanted to look through his phone, he'd hand it over. Hers was the same thing.

"What did it say?"

"You missed your appointment at the clinic yesterday," Koldan said quietly. "Not here, of course, but the place in Brooklyn. They're sending you a text confirmation to reschedule."

Oh.

Ana shrugged. "I don't want to reschedule. Just text back with a no on my end, okay?"

"Sure."

Something in the lilt of Koldan's tenor caught Ana's attention. She turned on the chaise, eyeing her usually charismatic and charming husband. He seemed quieter than normal, like something was going on in that head of his. Koldan could be odd like that—he often spent more time inside his head than he did outside. It also meant he was what Ana liked to call a deep thinker.

"What's wrong?" Ana asked.

"Aren't these notifications for your birth control shot?" Koldan asked, still looking down at Ana's phone.

"Yes."

"Huh."

"Koldan," Ana said, drawing his gaze to hers with his name.

"Yeah?"

"Don't overthink this."

Koldan's tongue peeked out to wet his lips. "I don't know if I can do that, Ana."

"There's no need to go looking for something that isn't there, Koldan. I think what it means is pretty obvious."

"Is it?"

"Yep," Ana said.

"Well, I guess we're not leaving the hotel today, either. Are we?"

Ana grinned. "Nope."

CHAPTER FIVE

"Adrik, Cora, wonderful to see you again," Christopher Marks said, shaking Adrik's hand before he gave Cora's outstretched one a kiss. Then, the man's gaze turned on Koldan and Ana. "And the newest addition to the Vasin family is here tonight, I see."

Ana supressed her shudder and did her best to offer the man a smile. "Nice to meet you, Senator."

Christopher smiled back. "Koldan, my boy, quite the wife you managed reel in. And from the Avdonin family, no less."

Koldan didn't blink a lash. "Well, I wasn't exactly aiming for a particular family when Ana came along."

"Sure you weren't," Christopher said like he didn't believe a word coming out of Koldan's mouth.

Ana held back her scoff, but only because Koldan's hand on her waist kept her grounded at his side. Politicians were sleazy as fuck. She didn't care what anyone had to say about it. It didn't matter who they were or what they were trying to sell, politicians could be bought and paid for by anyone with the right numbers in their bank account.

Christopher and Adrik were the perfect example. The Senator of New Jersey just happened to be firmly tucked in Adrik Vasin's back pocket. The Vasin family, running their own Bratva organization like Ana's father did, worked alongside officials and the most corrupt to get the best bang for their buck. It also helped to keep them out of trouble, Ana supposed.

In the end, it just made Ana feel like no politician of any sort could be trusted. Simple as that.

Unfortunately, living the kind of lifestyle they did often meant putting themselves into the public spotlight. Even growing up, with her father trying to keep his family out of the public view, Anton didn't always succeed. Sometimes, they embraced it, too, for charity events and things of that nature. Which was exactly why Ana had come with Koldan tonight. Although, it wasn't so much a charity event as a political rally for the Marks family. Another way to fill pockets and gain votes for the upcoming election. Ana had to put on her mask and play the proper part.

For Koldan, she didn't mind.

"And where is Sofia tonight?" the Senator asked.

"She's living in Brooklyn, now," Adrik answered.

"She didn't want to come?"

Adrik laughed. "My daughter was never one for these events."

"Ah, well, I'm aware," Christopher said. "But you know it looks good for her to be seen out and about with certain people just as the rest of your family is."

"Perhaps, but I think missing one will be fine," Adrik replied shortly.

Christopher waved a finger in the air, winking. "You know, that offer from my son is still on the table for her."

Koldan scoffed but hid it with his hand and the fakest cough Ana had ever heard. No one acted like they noticed Ana's husband's rudeness.

"That's never going to happen," Adrik said, smiling.

"She might change her mind," the senator replied.

"I doubt it," Cora muttered. "My daughter's stubbornness rivals even her father's, and that's saying something, believe me."

Ana forced herself not to laugh at the disgusted look on Cora Vasin's face. Koldan's mother wasn't Russian and really, Ana knew very little about her mother-in-law because of how private and quiet Cora was. Cora never once treated Ana like she wasn't welcomed or like she wasn't a part of the Vasin family, but breaking through the woman's tough-as-steel walls had been difficult.

Give it time, Ana told herself silently.

Ana and Koldan had only been married a couple of months. Before she moved to Jersey after their wedding, her meetings with Cora and Adrik were usually short and never too in-depth.

"Well, it would certainly benefit you, Adrik, if Sofia seriously considered Ryan's offer," Christopher said.

"What offer?" Ana asked Koldan, whispering so no one else would hear.

"Marriage," her husband replied.

Ana cringed nine ways to Sunday for Sofia. That would never happen. Sofia liked her freedom and tying herself down to one man was probably not going to happen anytime soon.

"For the political side of things, I mean," Christopher said, grinning. "After all, Ryan is slowing working his way into the scene, too. It won't be long before he's following his old man's footsteps. What would you give to have your daughter aligned with a Senator, Adrik? Your left arm, I bet."

Adrik's stony expression didn't change. "I'm sure."

He didn't sound like he particularly meant it.

"If she wanted to sleep beside a snake, there's a pet store right down the block," Ana said before she could stop herself.

All the conversation silenced instantly. Adrik's gaze cut to his new daughter-in-law like he couldn't believe what he just heard. Koldan choked on air, holding back laughter. Cora raised one of her perfectly manicured brows high, but said nothing.

The Senator, on the other hand, looked repulsed.

"I beg your pardon, Mrs. Vasin?" the Senator asked, a threatening edge sharpening his words.

Ana wished she could be surprised, but she wasn't.

Koldan stepped in front of Ana, protecting his wife from view. "Back off, Chris."

"That wife of yours—"

"Is just that, my wife," Koldan interrupted sharply. "Back off, I said."

With a huff and a muttered goodbye to Adrik, the Senator stomped off.

"Sorry," Ana said.

Koldan chuckled, his shoulders shaking. He turned to face his wife with a smug as fuck smile. "Are you?"

"No."

"I didn't think so," Koldan said.

"Politicians made me feel icky," Ana said.

"Me, too," Cora replied. She smiled at her husband. "See, I told you she would fit right in."

Ana laughed.

"Nothing he hasn't heard before," Adrik said, brushing it all off. "But next time, Ana, try to keep it inside your head or at least low enough so that he can't hear."

"I'll try," Ana said. "But he is a snake and I imagine so is his son."

"They are," her father-in-law agreed.

"Well done," Cora said, patting Ana's arm.

That was probably the most shocking of all. Ana returned her mother-in-law's smile and let Cora drag her off to find a server with wine.

CHAPTER SIX

Ana pushed open the office door to her husband's club and promptly froze right where she stood. Koldan, resting in his chair and overlooking what seemed to be paperwork on his desk, didn't take note of Ana's entrance. A woman sat on the edge of his desk wearing the tightest, shortest skirt Ana had ever seen. The female's high heel tapped a beat on the oak leg.

The girl was beautiful. She was blonde, green-eyed with makeup done flawlessly and legs for days. She held a magazine in her hand, looking it over while Koldan kept his head down on his work.

Jealousy and anger burned white-hot through Ana. She couldn't control it even if she tried. Never once had she ever thought Koldan would step out on their marriage—he wasn't that kind of man. But she didn't like the sight she was looking at.

"Koldan," Ana said, loud enough to catch her husband's, and the unknown woman's, attention.

Koldan glanced up, a smile splitting his lips. "Ana."

"Hey." Ana crossed her arms and eyed the female, not bothering to hide her contempt. "I thought you were busy today. Too busy to meet up for lunch, right?"

"I am."

"Oh?"

Koldan cocked a brow as the woman slid off his desk. "I have orders to fill. What's wrong with you?"

Ana met the woman's gaze as she said goodbye to Koldan and crossed the room. She brushed past Ana without a word, but didn't drop her stare. There was something behind those green eyes, something Ana didn't like or trust. Once the female was gone, Ana slammed the door.

"What in the hell was that?" Ana asked, waving in the direction the female had gone.

"My floor manager?" Koldan asked back, confused.

"Is that what she is?"

"Yes."

Ana nodded, refusing to let up in her defensive stance. "How often does she sit on your desk wearing a club dress and reading a magazine while you work, Koldan?"

Koldan's gaze narrowed and he cocked his head to the side. "Are you asking me if I'm fucking Mara?"

Great, the girl was Russian, too. Even better.

"Yes," Ana said simply. "I am."

"No, Ana. I'm not."

"Then why—"

"I was giving her the orders to make sure I hadn't missed something. It's a long process and she's been up here for a good two hours or more. In case you forgot, last week you cleared my office of all the furniture because you wanted to redecorate. She has no place to sit other than my lap and that's not going to happen."

Koldan's words had been spoken quietly but surely. Ana's anger dissipated, quickly turning into embarrassment.

"I just … it didn't look good," Ana settled on saying.

"I'm not that kind of man," Koldan replied.

She knew that, but sometimes …

"I trust you," Ana said instead of voicing her inner thoughts.

Koldan's brow furrowed. "I hope so. Otherwise, we're wasting a lot of time here."

"No, we're not wasting time."

"What was so important that you left your office to come find me here?" Koldan asked, pushing up from his leather chair. "Didn't you have a meeting with that new client for their penthouse or whatever?"

"I did, but I got a call and it was exciting. I wanted to tell you in person."

Ana took in the sight of her husband dressed in his usual slacks, silk shirt, and matching tie. Koldan preferred dark wash jeans and T-shirts at home, but outside, he was professional through and through. No one who ever met this man and didn't know him personally would ever think he was Russian Mafia bred. Koldan looked damn good—tall, dark and handsome.

In just a few short months, Koldan had changed in very visible ways to Ana. Before, he'd been so involved in the underbelly of the mob and the dirty work of it all, that Ana couldn't count the times on one hand she witnessed him sitting behind a desk or discussing business that wasn't Bratva related. But since they married and moved to Jersey, Koldan was settling into a different role. The business man, hardworking and dedicated, ruthless still, and charming as always.

She knew why, too, of course. Koldan was stepping more and more into his father's shoes for the Bratva, which meant he couldn't just be running the streets and the people on them like he had been before. He needed to be professional and quick, he needed to build an empire around himself and make his own name. One that reflected the man he was following but also put him front and center as his own man in the Bratva game.

Ana couldn't say she disliked the changes. It felt like a new step in their life.

"I love you," Ana said.

Koldan came to stand in front of Ana, tilting her chin up under his urging with two fingers. Before she could get another word in edgewise, Koldan's mouth crashed down on hers, taking away her ability to think or breathe. Everytime he kissed her, every sweep of his lips across hers and with every dive of his tongue, she felt owned by this man. No one else had ever been able to give Ana that feeling.

"I am not that kind of man," Koldan repeated as he pulled away, sweeping his thumb over her bottom lip.

"I know," Ana whispered. Her tongue darted out to touch his thumb still caressing her mouth. "I'm sorry."

But that girl still screamed bad news to Ana. She chose to drop it.

"And I love you, too," Koldan murmured.

Ana grinned. "Good."

"What was the news?"

"Oh! I almost forgot."

Koldan chuckled. "I'm very distracting."

She poked her husband in the stomach, feeling his hard muscles jump under her touch. "You are."

"The news?"

"Claire is pregnant. Demyan called to tell me," Ana explained.

Koldan's face lit up with a wide smile, but a sadness lingered in his gaze. They'd been trying for months to have a baby and nothing had happened yet. Ana didn't want to think that something might be wrong, but the what ifs still played around in her head.

"Is she?" Koldan asked.

"Yep. Not very far along, though, so we have to keep quiet about it until they're ready to tell the world."

Koldan nodded. "All right. Your mother and father must be happy."

"Probably. You were the first person I wanted to tell after I talked to my brother."

"Oh?"

"Yes." Ana caught his hand in hers and squeezed. "Come home with me."

"I have work, Ana."

She didn't care.

"So? End the day early. Come home. Please?"

Koldan sighed, eyeing the papers on his desk over his shoulder. "That means it'll be an early morning tomorrow, *krasivyy*."

"I'll wake you up in the way you like," Ana teased, leering.

And the way he liked just happened to be her mouth on his cock. Ana kind of loved waking him up like that, too.

Koldan smirked a sexy sight. "Deal."

CHAPTER SEVEN

Ana melted into the bed, feeling ticklish and giggly as Koldan's lips skimmed down her spine. There was something wicked and hot curling through her blood, thickening it and making her crazy.

"Stop giggling," Koldan demanded.

"I can't. That tickles."

"Oh, I think you can, *krasivyy*. And if not, I can always make you stop, Ana."

Ana liked the sound of that. "Can you?"

"Are you asking or wanting?" Koldan asked, his lips kissing across the spot where her ass melded into her lower back. Ana writhed into his touch. "Ana, talk to me."

"Wanting."

Christ, didn't he already know?

She always, always wanted when it came to him.

Ana felt breathless and spun. His one hand grabbed her ass and kneaded the flesh as his other dipped between her thighs to find what he wanted there. Ana sighed her pleasure into the pillow while Koldan's fingers swept between the fleshy lips of her sex and slid a line over her slit and straight up to her clit. When his digit came in contact with her clit, Ana couldn't help but push back into his hand.

Koldan's dark chuckles filled the quiet room. "So impatient, Ana."

"For you I am."

"Good things come to those who wait, *krasivyy*."

"Good things will certainly be coming soon if you bury those fingers of yours into my pussy, Koldan."

Her husband answered that statement by plunging two fingers straight into her core. Ana felt her walls clamp down around his sudden intrusion as her juices gushed. Moaning into the pillow, Ana gave herself over to Koldan's talented fingers that knew how to play her body just right without ever needing any direction from her.

"You're so fucking wet, Ana," Koldan ground out.

His teeth nipped into her ass cheek, making her yelp. It melted into a gasp when he curled his fingers at just the right angle with his next thrust to stimulate her G-spot. Ana felt her husband's mouth touch down at the base of her spine, over and over, higher and higher. His kisses made a path up to her shoulders where he lapped at her skin and hummed the sexiest sound.

"Come for me, *krasivyy*," Koldan ordered. "Let me feel you soaking my fingers before I really get us started."

Ana's body wasn't very far behind in answering his demand. With just the flick of his thumb pressing hard into her clit, she came undone. Bliss raged as she buried her scream into the pillow and fisted the bedsheets. Ana felt Koldan move back down her body as the waves crashed over her senses. Never once did his fingers stop or slow inside her pussy.

Without a word, Ana found herself flipped over to her back and staring into deep blue eyes. Something dark and promising swam behind Koldan's irises as he raked his gaze down her trembling, sweaty form. She didn't know how he was capable of doing it, but he always made her feel like every single inch of her was his just by looking at her.

"So beautiful," he murmured.

Ana let out a slow, shaky breath. "All yours."

"All mine."

Koldan grew quiet as he spread her thighs and fitted himself between her legs. One of her ankles hooked over his shoulder while he held the other in his strong grasp. His cock, hard and pulsing with his heartbeat, rested against her exposed sex. With a shift of his hips, Koldan was inside her.

Ana flexed upwards from the bed as he filled her entirely. Nothing ever felt quite as sublime and wonderful as Koldan's cock stretching her full and taking her entirely. Her sensitive pussy clenched around his length as he seated himself balls deep. Air cut through Ana's teeth like a cat's hiss.

"Beautiful," Koldan repeated.

A live wire. That's what she felt like. As if her nerves were exposed and snapping with electricity. Like she was going to burn into ashes beneath this man.

When he finally started to move, Ana let go again.

CHAPTER EIGHT

"**K**oldan," Ana said, her voice coming out faint and unsure.

Koldan didn't look up from the newspaper he was reading. "Yeah?"

Ana glanced at the plastic device in her hands. Month after month, nothing happened. She'd stopped worrying about it because they were young and healthy. It would come when it came.

"Ana, what is it?" Koldan asked.

She met his gaze from the kitchen entryway, wondering how to tell him. It was exciting and terrifying at the same time. It was new and beautiful … and holy shit.

Was she ready for this? Was she ready for what this meant?

She thought she was … before two little pink lines crossed a screen.

"Ana?"

"It's positive," Ana said quietly.

Koldan cocked his head to the side, his brow lifting high. "Positive? What is?"

"The pregnancy test."

The cup of coffee Koldan was holding dropped to the table with a bang. What little bit of liquid was left in the cup splashed over the marble top, but he didn't act like he'd noticed or cared. Ana had stopped telling him when she used a test because she just waited to see if her cycles came or didn't. This month, it hadn't. So, she went and picked up a test just to see.

"I'm pregnant," Ana whispered.

"Pregnant?" Koldan asked.

Ana nodded.

The widest, happiest smile graced Koldan's features. His arms flew wide as he stood from the chair. A loud whoop of excitement echoed through the house as he rounded the table and took a step toward her.

Ana was frozen in place.

"Pregnant?" he asked again.

"Yeah," Ana said, waving the test.

"Oh, my fucking God!"

She didn't get another word in edgewise. Koldan was there in front of her in a flash. Ana found herself buried into his embrace as he held her tight.

Pregnant …

CHAPTER NINE

"And?" Adrik asked pointedly. "Tell me what it is, now. I need to know."

"You can wait a few more minutes," Koldan said, waving his father off as he snatched a pickle from the middle of the table and handed it to Ana.

"I absolutely cannot!" Adrik muttered.

Ana stuck the pickle in her mouth and bit down on the sour food to keep from laughing at her father-in-law.

"You've waited four months so far," Koldan said.

"I didn't have a choice then," Adrik argued.

"Oh, well."

Adrik sighed. "He knew what time to call."

"Anton had something to deal with," Koldan explained. "Ana promised to tell him first. You wanted to know first. Compromise."

Koldan's hand found Ana's slightly rounded stomach. She sighed into the touch of her husband, feeling little flutters from the baby inside. At nearly five months along in her first pregnancy, things were going exceptionally well. The baby was on par and healthy. She wasn't too tired, and she managed to sleep well through the night. Koldan spoiled her more than ever. He was so proud that he was going to be a father.

Ana couldn't wait to see him with their little one.

Koldan was in love already.

Anton, on the other hand, was demanding Ana come home more often, but the two hour car drives were just a little too much for her to handle with the motion sickness she seemed to have. So, her father and mother had been making trips to Jersey instead. Ana figured that helped her papa to see what her life was like here, and how she was doing without him.

"Some compromise," Adrik said. "He wouldn't know."

Ana swallowed the last bit of her pickle. "He'd know."

"You think?" Adrik asked.

Cara laughed but hid it by raising her wine glass to her lips. Even Sofia rolled her eyes at her father's question.

"You have met my father, haven't you?" Ana asked.

Adrik didn't grace that with a response. It was self-explanatory enough. Anton Avdonin knew everything if he wanted to. Simple as that.

Ana's iPad dinged with an incoming message, and she knew that was the iMessenger. Bringing up the screen, she opened the video chat to see her mother and father as well as her brother, Vera and a very pregnant Claire sitting around the table. Ana set her own iPad in the middle of the table against a serving bowl. Everyone at the table moved so that they could be in frame, and the Avdonins could see them as well. Guessing by the fact Ana could see everyone in the frame from her father's side perfectly well, Anton had put his iPad high again.

That would be the third one he broke doing that.

"You shouldn't sit your iPad on the hearth, it might fall off," Ana told her father.

"Yes, Viviana," Anton said, as sarcastically as he could manage. "Thank you for the help."

Ana's mother snickered but stayed quiet.

Adrik smacked his palms to the table. "You're late, comrade."

Anton shrugged. "Vine made pie."

"Pie?" Adrik asked. "You made me wait for pie?"

"You should taste my wife's pie," Anton replied simply. "Maybe you would understand."

"Cora—"

"Doesn't cook," Cora interrupted her husband. "Don't even start, Adrik."

Adrik scowled. "Whatever. Are we ready?"

Ana giggled at the sight of her father's smirk.

"I would think so," Anton replied.

Ana looked to Koldan, who only shrugged in response.

"Don't leave me to do this alone," Ana said.

Koldan laughed. "Do you want me to do it, then?"

"Just tell me," Adrik said. "Pink or blue?"

"Blue," Ana and Koldan said together.

"A boy?" Anton asked. "Another?"

Claire was having a little boy, too, as far as Ana understood. They would be born only three months apart.

"A very healthy boy," Koldan confirmed.

Ana wasn't sure where all the noise came from between her family or Koldan's. But the cheers were goddamn deafening.

And lovely.

A boy.

"Ana, you're going to be fine," Anton said softly.

Fear crawled up Ana's spine like she'd never felt before. Never in her life had she ever felt so completely inadequate or incompetent at something. Shouldn't this sort of thing come natural to a person? You know, like once the little creature was inside a woman growing, that motherly instinct should somehow kick in and all that?

Apparently not for Ana.

"I don't know—"

"Yes, you do," Anton interjected firmly.

"Papa, listen to me for five seconds."

Anton sighed harshly on the other end of the line. "Fine, Ana. Get it out."

"What if I just … fail?" Ana asked.

"At being a mother?"

"Well … yeah."

"Ana, my God," Anton mumbled.

Okay, so when she put in that way, it kind of sounded stupid.

"You're going to be a great mother, my *dushka*," Anton said firmly. "I know you're scared because this is new and you're getting close to the end of the pregnancy, but you can't get sucked into that nonsense right now. You have better, far more important things to worry about. You will know what to do and you will feel if something isn't right, Ana."

"But I don't feel like a mom," Ana said quietly.

"Do you know when I felt like a father?" Anton asked instead of responding to Ana's statement.

"When?"

"When I held Demyan for the first time. I looked down at him, and he had his eyes wide open, looking right back at me. I could see me all through him and I knew he was mine, and I was his. In that second, he was my boy and I was his father. No two people are the same, Ana. You're scared and worrying over nothing, sweetheart. Rest and let that husband of yours take care of you while you can enjoy being pampered and spoiled with what time you have left alone."

"I want to be a good mother," Ana said.

"You will be. After all, you had the best mother to learn from, Ana."

She had.

CHAPTER TEN

Pain coursed through Ana's system. She breathed through it, or tried, anyway. Over and over, unrelenting and constant, the pain continued. It felt like her insides were being ripped out and then stuffed back in again for a few minutes before the process started itself all over.

Nobody prepared a woman for this.

Saying it hurt wasn't enough.

Labor was hell.

Ana had been in the midst of hers for thirteen hours with no immediate end in sight.

Whining, Ana let all the air out of her chest and sucked in another big breath. Tears tracked fat lines down her cheeks. She was sure her hair and face was a goddamn mess. She held onto anything that she could for dear life as the contractions ripped through her body.

"It is not like a wave," Ana muttered.

Koldan laughed bleakly. "No?"

"No," Ana cried, shaking her head. "It is nothing like a wave. Fucking liars."

Someone had told her to think of the contractions like a wave that would come in slowly, reach a peak, and then decline. They lied, the bastards. Ana's contractions just felt the same all the way through each two damned minutes of one.

Pain medication had been offered. Ana refused. Women had been doing this very thing for thousands of years, after all. Why couldn't she do it, too? Ana was seriously starting to regret that decision.

"Tell me what you want," Koldan whispered. "Or what you need, Ana. Anything."

Ana felt her husband's forehead press to hers. His lips ghosted over her trembling, dry ones. They were alone in their private hospital room. The nurses would come in every so often to check Ana and offer her medication. The last time, she'd demanded they leave her alone unless she called for them. At least until she wasn't so agitated.

"Ana, please," Koldan said.

She melted into the feelings of his thumbs rolling over her cheeks with the softest pressure. He'd not left her side even once. She knew he was having a hard time because she was in pain and he couldn't take it away. That was the kind of man Koldan was.

He never wanted Ana to suffer for anything.

"I want my mom," Ana said, barely above a breath.

Not her father or one of her close friends. No, her mom. Because Viviana had been here and she had done this. And sometimes, girls just needed their fucking mothers.

And right now … at almost twenty-six-years-old, Ana needed hers.

Koldan's gaze dropped from hers, his shoulders slumping. "You know I can't do that, *krasivyy*."

Viviana and Anton had taken a trip out of town for the weekend. With two weeks to go on her due date, no one thought Ana's first pregnancy would go early. Everyone, even her doctors, thought she would go overdue by several days, as was the norm with first pregnancies. Viviana was supposed to come up the following week and stay with Ana so she could go in to the hospital with her.

The baby had other plans.

No one seemed to be able to get a hold of Ana's parents. Demyan was making the trip to Vermont to the secluded cabin, but chances were, that would take several more hours before her brother would be able to get her parents back. The baby boy would probably already be born.

"I really want my mom," Ana said, feeling another fresh line of tears track down her cheeks.

Koldan blew out a heavy breath. "Five minutes, okay? Just give me five minutes and I'll be back."

Ana didn't want him to go anywhere, but she nodded anyway. With another kiss to Ana's sweaty forehead, Koldan left the private hospital room. Somehow, Ana managed to get off the godforsaken hospital bed that was doing nothing to help her. Crouched low to the floor with her palms on the cold tiles, Ana breathed her way through another wave of pain and sadness.

She didn't hear the hospital door open a second time. She didn't hear anything until Cora Vasin was crouching down in front of Ana and holding her face in her hands. Ana stared at her mother-in-law, feeling incapable and overwhelmed.

"You're doing great," Cora said, her voice uncharacteristically soft.

"It hurts," Ana said.

That was all she could really think to say.

"It does," Cora agreed. "A lot. People lie all the time. You don't forget. But you'll be fine. What you don't need to do right now is panic or worry about things you can't control. What can you control right now, Ana?"

Her breathing. Her feelings. The people around her and things in the room like the lighting and sound. The more Ana thought about it, the more she realized there was a lot she could control to make this situation easier.

Ana stayed quiet.

"I know I'm not your mother, but I will stay until she gets here," Cora said.

"She might not get here," Ana whispered.

"Then I will stay."

Ana felt Koldan's hand touch her back before he was kneeling behind her. He wrapped his arms around her shoulders, leaned his head to the back of her neck, and rocked her back and forth.

"You're doing great," Cora repeated. "What do you need right now, Ana?"

Her mother.

But Cora was good, too.

"Pain meds," Ana settled on saying.

Koldan chuckled.

Even Cora laughed. "I think we can do that."

CHAPTER ELEVEN

Ana felt like a mother when she heard her son cry for the first time. It was like an instant shot of understanding, love, and need straight into her heart. Nothing was ever as perfect or as beautiful as that one little sound had been. And when she held him, wrapped in fluffy blankets and still dirtied from being taken from his happy home, Ana decided the pain was worth it.

Because she did something amazing.

Adrik Nicoli was an easy child. He didn't fuss or make a lot of noise. He was most happy in his mother's arms, but he had an obvious attachment to his father, as well. Koldan planned on thoroughly spoiling his first son. It didn't matter what Ana or anyone else said, Adrik was Koldan's golden child. The boy could do no wrong.

Well, to Ana, Adrik could do no wrong, either.

"My God, he's gotten big," Viviana said.

Ana watched her eighteen-month-old toddler run after his grandfather in the back yard. Anton hid behind a tree and then popped right back out, making Adrik fall back to his butt on the grass. The toddler squealed loudly as Anton tickled the boy from his kicking legs all the way up to his belly.

"He's growing fast," Ana agreed with her mother.

"He eats all the damn time," Koldan put in, laughing.

"Nothing wrong with that," Claire said as she came to stand in front of the table with a tray full of glasses and juice. "Just means he's healthy."

Even Demyan had taken time out of his schedule to come over to visit with Ana, Koldan, and little Adrik. A smiling, grinning Roman sat on his quiet father's lap. Demyan had been playing a game where he bounced Roman over and over and sang a song of some sort. Roman had his father doing the game for thirty minutes nonstop.

"Again," Roman demanded in that childish voice of his.

Demyan shook his head, chuckling. "You're making my knee tired, Rome."

"GRANDPAPA!" Roman cried. "PAPA SAID NO!"

"Jesus," Demyan muttered under his breath, dropping Roman to the ground. "Go, little man."

Roman scampered off to Anton's side. Without leaving either child out of the game, Anton managed to wrangle Roman into the tickle fest, too. It was so unusual for Ana to think of her father as a former crime boss when she saw him now like he was with the kids.

Only one thing mattered to her father: his family.

"He is so spoiled," Demyan said, sighing.

"You love it," Claire replied, grinning.

Demyan didn't say a word but he caught his wife around the waist and pulled her into his lap.

"You think he's bad, you should have seen you when you were that age," Viviana said, smirking. "If there's anything Anton does best, it's spoil kids. It's too late to save Roman, Demyan. Just grin and bear it."

Demyan shook his head. "You're awful, Ma."

"I know."

"He's a good kid," Demyan said, resting back in his chair. "A little high strung, but good."

"I don't know where he gets that from," Claire said.

"Anton," Viviana muttered.

Laughter rung out over the backyard.

"Where is Vera?" Ana asked.

Demyan scowled. "Ballet."

Claire smacked his leg. "Stop it. You know she loves that school."

"I know," Demyan said, his voice heavy. "But they're hard on her. If she misses a step, they're right on her ass. I can't sit there and watch it without needing to hold myself back from breaking someone's fucking neck."

"I know it's not the same thing, but competitive swim training was hard, too, Demyan," Ana told her brother. "The coaches—or teachers—are there to push you to be better. If she's going to make a career out of dancing someday, the harsher the teacher, the better."

"I still don't like it," Demyan replied.

Yeah, Ana supposed he wouldn't. Demyan had always been a little overprotective when it came to Vera.

Ana felt Koldan's hand slip into hers. Silently, he tugged her closer into his side. Content there, Ana took in Koldan's warmth, silent strength, and love.

"So, when are you two planning on telling the rest of the world?" Viviana asked, never taking her eyes off her husband and the kids.

"Tell you what?" Ana asked.

Viviana smiled. "You know what."

Ana tried to seem dumb. "No, I don't."

Butterflies beat around in her stomach. Nervousness had never worked out well for Ana.

"What, Ma?" Demyan asked.

"Ana is pregnant," Viviana said.

Koldan's arm tightened around Ana's waist. Ana wondered how her mother could possibly know that. She was only a couple of months along in her second pregnancy and she certainly didn't look pregnant.

"Mothers know," Viviana said before Ana could ask.

"Or someone else spilled their guts," Ana said, giving Koldan a look.

"I said nothing," Koldan murmured before kissing her lips quickly.

Heat and desire swirled around Ana's insides. Her second pregnancy was turning out to be different in the way that it took barely any prodding at all and her libido was up and revving, demanding attention. Koldan was more than happy to feed into that need, thankfully. Unfortunately, this was not the right time or place.

"Stop," Ana whispered at the sight of Koldan's growing, knowing smirk.

"So, when?" Viviana asked again.

Ana laughed lightly. "Why should I tell you anything? You just did it for me."

"A girl this time, maybe?" Viviana's smile was almost conspiratorial in nature. "You can name her after me."

Ana guffawed at her mother. "What about *my* name?"

"You were named after me … and your grandmother, but me, too."

Koldan hummed, dotting kisses along Ana's cheekbone as he said, "I don't know how well I would do with a girl. Let's just say I'm hoping for a second boy."

Ana poked her husband's stomach. "We might have a girl."

"Nope, God's only gonna give me boys, Ana. It's decided."

Oh, was it now?

CHAPTER TWELVE

"Ah, the little boss's wife is in the house tonight, I see."

Ana turned at the sound of the gravelly voice. A large, overweight man with a loosened tie and a wrinkled suit sauntered over to their table. His voice held the distinct accent of a Russian's, but Ana didn't recognize the man, as far as that went. When it came to Koldan and his work, Ana tried to stay out of it.

She wasn't stupid. She knew Koldan was a brigadier—a Captain—for his father's Bratva and that he often acted as Adrik's right-hand man in most things where business was concerned. Koldan never pretended to hide the things he was involved in, but he always made sure to keep Ana at a safe distance away from the men he controlled and the darker side of business.

Ana didn't mind, really.

"And getting larger by the day, I must say," the man said, looking Ana's rounded stomach over.

Ana's hand fluttered up to her midsection, unnerved by the man looking at her. Sitting at the club's table with a few of Koldan's men while her husband dealt with some issue in the backroom didn't bother Ana. Koldan wouldn't leave her alone, especially not pregnant, with people he didn't trust. But the guys were lost in conversation and gawking over the girls working the floor and serving drinks.

This man, however, Ana didn't trust at all.

"Hello," Ana said to the man.

"Hey there, pretty face," the man muttered. "You're Anton's kid, yeah?"

Ana felt dirty as the man looked her up and down again. After her rape years ago, it took Ana a long time to feel completely comfortable in an enclosed space with men she didn't know well. But once she had jumped over that hurdle, the anxiety rarely reared its ugly head.

The panic seemed to be thumping right in her throat at this man.

"Anton is my father," Ana replied.

"Good man," the guy said. "Damn good boss, but that boy of his … Demyan … he's a nasty fucker. He's the boss now, yeah?"

Ana didn't answer that question. Apparently, the guy wasn't looking for one. Leaning down over the table, he reached out and caught one of Ana's stray curls in his fingers. Tugging just enough for it to hurt, the man grinned.

"Good to see Koldan's doing something right—he's got you knocked up, prettied up, and sat down to be admired by the rest of us. Seems the boy does know what to do with a wife like you." He tugged again on her hair and said, "But we all know that with a little liquor, you're just the kind of girl who'll give a man whatever he wants, right? What was his name … Cavan, was it?"

Ana jerked away from him, a pain splintering in her chest at the sound of her rapist's name. How and why did this man know that? "What in the fuck are you doing? Don't put your hands on me! Get the hell away from me or I'll make sure my husband has the pleasure of cutting your dick off and shoving it up your own ass."

Finally, the other men at the table seemed to notice Ana's predicament.

"Mud, didn't Koldan say you weren't welcomed back until you cleaned up your shit and opinions?" Ana's bull for the night asked.

Mud—*odd name*, Ana thought—shrugged. "Just came to meet his wife. Heard he brought her in for the boys to gawk at."

Ana swallowed hard, feeling something awful well in her gut. It was Koldan's birthday and he had to work late because of some shipment or truck of shit he needed to handle. Ana convinced him to let her tag along for the night so that he wouldn't have to spend the majority of his birthday without her.

With a sharp order in Russian from Ana's bull, Mud disappeared back into the crowd of club goers. Not three minutes later, Koldan was sitting back at the table. As they usually did when they went out together and were seen in a space where other Bratva was present, Koldan was careful not to shower too much affection on Ana. She understood why—because it wasn't safe for him to show where his weaknesses were.

Even still, under the table as he talked to the man at his other side, Koldan's finger drew soft, tantalizing pathways on Ana's exposed leg. It was just one of the ways he always let her know that he was there, loving her and wanting her.

Despite being eight months along in her second pregnancy and feeling like a giant balloon, Koldan never made Ana feel like anything less than beautiful and sexy to him. Even with the young, gorgeous women working around them and the ones dancing and drinking on the floor, Ana's husband didn't give them a single ounce of his attention.

She still felt sick in the seat, unsure if she should tell Koldan what happened before he arrived back at the table. She would tell him, to be sure, but not when his men were around. Ana didn't want to seem like some petty, frightened wife. A person's character and reputation was everything in the Bratva world. A man like Koldan couldn't have a wife who needed coddled from all the bad things in life. His wife needed to appear as strong as him in all things and at all times.

Ana didn't need to tell Koldan a thing, apparently.

"Who?" Koldan demanded.

The bull muttered something in Russian. Ana wished she had taken the time to learn more of her family's second language growing up than just the little bit she did.

Koldan pushed out of the booth, turned, and offered Ana his hand without a word. She stared at it, confused. "Come."

"Don't you have that truck to handle when it comes in?" Ana asked.

"I have men for that. Come, Ana."

Ana took Koldan's hand and let him help her out of the booth. Without a word, he placed his palm over her stomach, put his other hand to her lower back, and directed her through the crowd of people, keeping her close to his side.

Lowly, Koldan asked, "Are you okay?"

"Fine," Ana assured.

"What did he say to you?"

"He asked about Anton and Demyan."

"What else?" her husband pressed.

"He asked about Cavan and he made a remark that seemed like I asked for what happ—"

Ana didn't get to finish her sentence. Koldan spun her around so that they were facing one another. In the dark back hallway, no one could see them though she could still hear the sounds of the music and people.

"Don't you dare," Koldan growled.

"I don't think that," Ana said, recognizing the anger in Koldan's stare. It wasn't often they talked about Cavan Dolan or Ana's rape. They didn't have to, really. It happened and she'd dealt with it through therapy and time.

Eventually, she moved on. It was her past but it didn't define her future. "You know I don't blame myself."

Koldan weaved their fingers together and tugged Ana closer. "I think I'm going to send you home with a bull. Okay?"

"Why?" Ana asked.

"Because I have something to deal with," Koldan replied simply.

Ana didn't feel like she had to ask, but she did anyway. "That man?"

"Has seen his last day."

"You can just … let it go, Koldan."

Koldan's mouth drew into a tight, unhappy line. "No, *krasivyy*, I can't. Letting someone off with behavior like that is asking for trouble. If I allow even one man to disrespect my wife in front of others, I'm allowing every man the same permission. Don't wait up for me, okay?"

Nothing she would say could make a difference. Sometimes, this was just how their world worked. She was Koldan's unrelenting cornerstone—she would support and stand by his side no matter what he did. He needed that from her and she was more than happy to give it. It didn't matter to her if she didn't like all of the things he did. She didn't have to like them.

Because she loved him.

Entirely.

Ana smiled, shrugging. "I'm still going to wait up for you."

Koldan bent his head down just far enough to capture her lips with his. "Yeah, I know."

CHAPTER THIRTEEN

The sound of running water woke Ana. Blinking away the sleepiness in her vision, she glanced around the dark bedroom. A light filtered out from under the door connecting the bedroom to the master bath. Adrik barely stirred next to his mother as Ana pushed the blanket away and stood from the bed.

Apparently Ana had been more tired than she thought if she had fallen asleep waiting for Koldan. Pregnancy could do that. Plucking up Adrik from the bed, she smiled as the toddler snored against his mother's shoulder. She walked him to his bedroom and put him in his small bed, covering him up snug under his Thomas the Train blankets.

Making her way back to the master bedroom, Ana wondered why Koldan hadn't woken her up himself after he got home. Ana knocked on the bathroom door, hearing Koldan's quiet cuss on the other side.

"Go to bed, Ana," Koldan said loud enough for her to hear.

Something in the lilt of his tone brokered no room for argument. That told Ana she couldn't let it go. Well, she wasn't going to now.

"Open up, Koldan."

"Ana—"

As far as privacy went, Ana respected her husband's need for it. He never stepped over her personal lines, and she tried to never step over his. Turning the handle on the bathroom door, she could tell it wasn't locked. Ana pushed the door open to find Koldan standing against the marble sink with his hands under running water.

His back was tense and even the muscles in his arms looked tight and taut, like he was holding something back. Anger flashed in his gaze as he turned to look at Ana, but it disappeared just as fast. He still wore his clothes from earlier, though his suit jacket was resting over the side of the counter.

"Hey, what's wrong?" Ana asked.

"Please get out."

"No."

Koldan sighed, shaking his head. "You're too stubborn for your own good sometimes, *krasivyy*."

"You married me."

"I did, but that doesn't mean you don't frustrate me sometimes, Ana. I love you, but God knows your stubbornness could test the patience of even a Saint."

Ana shrugged, leaning against the doorframe. "Makes for a good marriage."

"Actually, it makes for a good woman," Koldan muttered.

He hissed as he pulled his hands out from the running water and covered them with a towel. He turned just enough to give Ana a good look at the splatters of red dotting over the front of his silk shirt and down his stomach. Some of the red dots had skipped under his jaw and over his chin.

Ana stared at her husband, confused. "Is that blood?"

Koldan's jaw tensed. "Yes."

"Oh, Koldan."

"I told you to go back to bed."

Maybe she should have.

"Do we have any antibiotics?" her husband asked. "Or a cream, maybe."

Ana's brow furrowed. "Why?"

"Just because."

"Because *why*, Koldan?"

"I split my knuckles all over that idiot's teeth and I don't know what kind of diseases he might have had in his dirty mouth. Do we or don't we?"

Ana let out a slow breath, massaging her temples with her fingers. "We do."

Of course, they did. They had a toddler son that always managed to get at least one scraped knee or elbow a week.

"Where?"

Stepping away from the door, Ana walked across and opened up the cabinet beneath the sink. She pulled out a first aid kit and searched for the antibiotic cream she knew was in there. Once she had it, she set it on the counter and waved at Koldan.

"Take the damn towel off and let me see them," Ana ordered.

Koldan shook his head. "I'll do it, babe. It's fine."

"Koldan, please don't make me say it again. I'm tired and pregnant and not in the mood. Let me clean your knuckles so I can go to bed, and you can apologize to me in the morning."

With a disgruntled grunt, Koldan flung the towel covering his hands to the counter. Ana's chest ached at the sight of his knuckles. They were red, cut on every single one, and swollen. They looked terribly sore. Ana ghosted her fingers around the injuries, noting how his hands stayed steady at the same time.

"Does it hurt?" she asked.

"Barely," Koldan muttered. "Felt especially good while I doled out the punishment, though."

Quietly, Ana went about cleaning Koldan's hands and applying the antibiotic cream. All the while, her husband watched her through his dark lashes, saying nothing.

"You don't have to break the face of every man who hurts me, Koldan," Ana said.

"Yes, I absolutely do."

Ana wished he wouldn't, though. "But—"

"I do, Ana," Koldan interrupted before she could get out another word. "Because you're mine—every single person needs to know it. And nobody gets to hurt what's mine, not unless they want to bleed for it, too."

CHAPTER FOURTEEN

Daniil Koldan was nothing like his older brother. He was fussy at night, demanding to sleep between his mother and father. From the very start, he was a momma's boy through and through. He liked all the attention he could get, and Ana didn't mind giving her little prince exactly what he deserved.

"Look at him," Koldan whispered.

Ana watched her husband trace the sleeping baby's features. Gently, he touched Daniil's little nose and lips. Daniil looked so much like his father, it was unreal. Even the set of his tiny cheekbones and the shape of his eyes were similar. Two-year-old Adrik shared both his mother and father's features, but Daniil took after Koldan entirely.

"He's so much quieter when he sleeps," Koldan said.

Ana laughed softly. "I know."

Leaning over, Koldan caught Ana's chin between his forefinger and thumb, bringing her closer for a kiss that seared her from the inside out. "I'm sorry, *krasivyy*."

Ana blinked, surprised. "For what?"

"I've been gone a lot, I know. I'm sorry for that. I'll try to be home more often."

"It's okay," she said. "If I was having trouble, I'd tell you."

Koldan grinned. "But I miss you, babe."

Ana kissed him again, letting her tongue war with his. Pulling away, she murmured, "I've missed you, too."

Koldan had a lot going on. Work in the Bratva never ended and now that he had officially dropped the brigadier title to stand at Adrik's side, more and more eyes were watching them both. Ana had a whole new level of respect for her mother. Being the Bratva wife was not easy. It was difficult to appear unaffected and cold at every turn. It was hard to keep your weak spots hidden. Ana had always been treated like royalty in her father's Bratva family, but this felt different in a way. Like she was being tested and gaged by the men under Koldan. Like they were wondering if she was a worthy partner for a man of his status.

Ana wasn't accustomed to that.

Koldan's attention went right back to their son. "I told you he was going to be a boy. No girls for me, Ana. Good thing. I don't know if I could handle boyfriends and dates."

"Periods, too," Ana added.

"Jesus. Boys only."

Ana smacked his arm lightly. "Well, I think I'm done giving you babies, anyway. So, you have your boys, Koldan."

"Our boys," he replied.

"Ours."

"And this little one is such a momma's boy," Koldan said, chuckling.

"I like him that way," Ana replied.

"One more?" he asked.

"One more what?"

"Baby."

Ana scoffed. "Not anytime soon, Koldan."

Koldan winked at her but didn't press her on the topic. Without a word, her husband plucked the sleeping child off the bed and cradled him in his arms.

"What are you doing?" Ana asked.

"Taking him to his bed," Koldan said.

"But he doesn't sleep in there."

Koldan looked down at Daniil. "He's sleeping now, Ana."

"He'll wake up."

A shrug answered her back. "Maybe, but I'll go in and rock him back to sleep."

Ana's heart melted a little more. Her husband was a great father. Hands on with their kids and he never shied away from parenting. "I don't mind him sleeping in here, Koldan."

"I do. Tonight, anyway."

"What, why?"

Koldan had never said anything of the sort before.

"You had your twelve week check-up the other day, didn't you?" her husband asked, grinning slyly.

Ana's body heated at his vaguely suggestive words. "I did."

"And?"

"All is good."

Koldan flashed his white teeth in a wickedly sinful smile. "Good. Go get in the bath, Ana. Relax for a little while or something."

Ana heard the telltale sounds of Daniil's cries the moment Koldan took him out of their bedroom. With a roll of her eyes, Ana pushed out of the bed and padded through to the master bath. If her husband wanted to play daddy for the night and rock their son to sleep a half of a dozen times, more power to him.

Ana didn't mind the break.

With a bath drawn and bubbles giving off the sweetest scent of vanilla and sugar, Ana undressed and climbed into the tub. The hot water instantly loosened the knots tightening her muscles. She hadn't realized how much stress her body was under until the water soothed it away. Forgetting where she was for a moment, Ana nearly dozed off in the hot, comforting bath.

A gentle graze of something warm and soft against her neck broke her from the daze. Confused, she blinked up at her husband's sensual smile.

"Fell asleep, hmm?" Koldan asked.

Had she?

"The water is still warm," Ana said, laughing lowly. "Must not have been for long."

"Took me twenty minutes to get him back to sleep. How hot was the water, Ana?"

"Hot enough." Ana flicked her wet wrist in Koldan's direction, splattering water and bubbles at him. "Get in with me."

"Oh, I can't deny you anything, Ana. Not when you look like that."

Ana grinned, thoroughly enjoying the show as Koldan undressed down to nothing but his skin and slipped into the large bathtub beside his wife. It was one of the things she loved the most about their home. Their Jacuzzi style tub provided more than enough room to fit two or three people side by side comfortably.

Resting her head on Koldan's shoulder, Ana felt what lingering tension she might have had fade away. "How was work?"

"Busy. How was the baby today?" he asked back.

Ana laughed. "Busy."

"I bet. My little monsters."

"I miss my studio and the clients, though," Ana added. "But I think I'd miss the kids more."

Koldan's hand found the spot under Ana's chin. He tilted her face up so he could look down at her. "What's going on in that head of yours?"

"I went to school for a long time to do what I do, and I enjoy designing homes."

"So?"

"So, maybe I have two kids and I don't want them raised by nannies or daycares, Koldan."

"Oh," her husband murmured. "This is entirely up to you, Ana. I won't mind either way."

"Promise?"

Koldan chuckled deeply, the sound rocking straight through Ana's chest. "Babe, I'm not going to lie here. I prefer you home with the kids, here when I need you, and up with me in the morning. But I also like it when you're doing what you want to do. I'd never take that away or ask you to give it up."

"I know."

It was one of the things she loved the very most about her husband.

"So, I'm just going to support you with whatever, Ana," Koldan said. "If that's giving up the studio office and the clients to stay at home with the boys, then so be it. If that's continuing on with your career, that's what it is."

Ana smiled. "I love you."

"I love you, too, *krasivyy*." Koldan's gaze raked down Ana's chest, making her shiver under the intensity. "And you're so beautiful."

"Am I?"

"Absolutely."

Ana didn't think she needed to question him on that. Koldan wasn't the kind of man who lied. Being naturally athletic allowed Ana to keep up her figure even through the pregnancies and the postpartum periods afterward. She took pride in her body, but she wasn't vain about it.

Nonetheless, it was always nice to hear her husband say it.

"Still get me harder than steel just by being close, Ana," Koldan murmured.

"Oh?"

Just to test if his words were indeed fact, Ana sought his cock out under the bubbly water. She found his member hard and thick in her palm as she stroked his length slowly. Koldan licked his lips and bent down to kiss Ana as she continued jerking him off. The gentle kiss quickly deepened when Ana parted her lips to allow her husband in. Koldan's tongue struck hard against hers as his hand slipped between her thighs.

"Oh, God," Ana whispered.

With just the touch of his hand to her sex, she was already burning up. He worked her sex with one finger as she stroked his dick harder, faster. Then, he added a second finger to Ana's pussy, stretching her open. No pain answered the hard drives of his fingers, just bliss and need. Sparks of her orgasm were already twisting inside her womb, promising release.

"Missed touching you," Koldan mumbled against her lips. "Feeling you, tasting you. Fuck, Ana, you're going to make me come … slow down."

Ana refused to relent. Koldan didn't give her a choice. His hand left her sex, so he could grab her around the waist and pull her into his lap. His cock pressed to her stomach as he kissed her hard and deep, his teeth scraping to her lips and making her gasp. Ana sighed when Koldan's fingers drove into her hair and pulled gently enough to make her feel the sting. His lips traveled down over her chin and neck to her chest. He took one of her nipples in his mouth. His tongue flatten to the rose bud before his teeth tightened around the nipple.

"Fuck," Ana hissed.

"That's the plan, georgous girl. I want you coming on my cock in the next two minutes and then I want you on the bed, ass up, and begging like I know you can. How does that sound?"

Good God.

"Perfect," Ana mumbled as Koldan situated his cock between her thighs. "So perfect."

Koldan chuckled but it melted into a groan as his cock pressed into her entrance. He filled her entirely, slowly. Ana's body took a second to adjust to her husband's girth and length but once she was, there was nothing but pleasure licking around her senses.

"Fuck me," Ana demanded.

Koldan grinned, sexy and lazy. "Whatever you want, princess."

His hands grabbed her waist tight. Lifting her off his cock, he dropped her back down just as fast. A full body shudder worked its way over Ana. Koldan grunted a sexy sound, driving her body into his again.

"Love your body," Koldan said, his teeth gritted and his eyes darkening.

Water sloshed out of the tub as she rode him faster, needing more. Koldan let her take the lead and grabbed her backside roughly, pulling her into him harder with their rhythm. It didn't take Ana long to remember their old tune. Making love with her husband, had always been like music to her. A song she couldn't forget. The very best melody ringing through her veins.

"Oh," Ana breathed, not feeling her orgasm until it was rushing through. "*Koldan.*"

"Fuck," her husband mumbled, squeezing her tighter.

Ana felt his cock pulse deep inside her flexing pussy, releasing his come. She fell into his wet chest, letting him hold her as they fell quiet.

"Missed this," Ana whispered as Koldan's hands found her hips.

Koldan kissed her chin softly. "Me, too."

"*Mmm.*" Ana hummed and wiggled in his lap, feeling his still semi-hard cock twitch inside her. "You wanted something else, didn't you?"

Koldan laughed dark and sexy, making Ana shiver. "To the bed."

"Ass up," she said, grinning.

CHAPTER FIFTEEN

Sofia Vasin looked damn good for being thirty-four, almost thirty-five. Even Ana was a little bit jealous at how her sister-in-law didn't seem to age a day. Wearing a tight club dress with heels sky high, Sofia drew the gazes of several men as she and Ana walked into the joint.

"Sofia," a familiar bouncer drawled, grinning salaciously. "Good to see your beautiful face in this place tonight. And how is the Vasin princess doing tonight, sweetheart?"

"Fantastically," Sofia replied, smirking. "How're you doing, Pete?"

"Better now that you graced my night."

"Flattery will get you everywhere."

Pete laughed. "Oh, I know exactly where it gets me. You looking for your brother?"

"We are," Sofia said.

"He's in the VIP with his guys."

"Thank you," Sofia said.

Pete nodded to Ana. "Ana."

"Pete," Ana greeted with a smile.

The bouncer knew better than to go off half-cocked with his flirtatious self on Ana. Koldan wouldn't stand for that shit, and the bouncer liked his job. As Sofia walked through the entryway that led to the main floor of the club, she breathed deep.

"Ah, the smell of drunk people first thing in the morning," Sofia said.

Ana scoffed. "It's ten at night."

"Morning for me, babe."

"Still haven't found a man to tie you down, huh, Sofia?" Ana asked.

Sofia shrugged. "He'd have to be one hell of a man, Ana. So far, I've found that whatever a man can do for me, I can do it myself, too."

"Except love."

"I do love me," Sofia said, winking.

"I mean for someone else to love you."

Sofia bumped Ana's hip with hers. "I know what you mean, smartass. I'm just …"

"What?" Ana asked.

"Not at that place in my life just yet, you know?"

"Not really." Ana couldn't imagine her life without her sons and Koldan. The amount of love in their home was astounding. She wouldn't give it up for the world. "My boys are everything to me, Sofia. I can't even think of something different. It doesn't feel right."

Sofia smiled. "You're a good mom. I'm happy my brother found someone like you, truly. Koldan is a special kind of guy. He's not like a lot of these guys," Sofia said, nodding toward the VIP section filled with younger and older men. Some Ana recognized, some she didn't. She couldn't spot her husband in the mix no matter how hard she tried to look. "Bratva, I mean. Koldan just turned out different. He gives a fuck. He cares. And he's got a decent respect for women, which is a lot more than some of these guys can say."

"I agree."

"Comes from our mother," Sofia said. "Well, his mom."

"She's yours, too," Ana pointed out.

Sofia nodded. "She is. And I love her. But Koldan … They always had a different kind of relationship—a closer one, maybe. I never felt left out, but they just connect on a different level. Maybe like the one I connect with Adrik on."

"Koldan loves his father," Ana replied.

"Very much. But he holds back with our dad, too. And I get that because sometimes I'm like that with Ma. Koldan adores our mother. Cora raised him to think beyond just his wants and needs. She made sure he understood that when he loved a woman, she should be the most important thing in his life. You should thank her, Ana. Koldan turned out pretty damn well. Ma figured he would needed a special kind of woman to fit him in this lifestyle, too. So she made damn sure when he went looking, he found the right one."

"He's a different breed," Ana said.

"Yeah, that sounds about right. But for me, I have no interest in being that for someone, Ana. I don't want babies. I love my nephews just like they're mine, anyway. I'm good like this." Sofia laughed lightly. "Don't worry about me being lonely or turning into some spinster."

"Adrik would love to see you settle down."

"Maybe I'll find a man someday who makes me want to do that with him, but today is not that day, Ana. And tonight …" Sofia trailed off, leering at the young man blocking the VIP section to keep anyone from entering the space. "Tonight, there is fresh meat in the house. I wouldn't mind sinking my teeth into that. Damn."

Ana laughed. "Christ, what are you, a fucking shark that smells blood in the water from miles away?"

"Just about."

"Be nice and don't get the poor guy in trouble, Sofia," Ana said, keeping her voice low. "I think he's one of Koldan's younger guys. Trying to make his way or earn his stars … or whatever."

Sofia pouted. "Boo."

"You're terrible."

"I know," Sofia said happily.

The man blocking the VIP section stepped aside to allow Ana and Sofia through.

"You didn't tell me your brother was going to be here tonight," Sofia said.

"Huh?" Ana followed her sister-in-law's gaze to find Demyan sitting on a leather bench alongside Koldan. The two men had their heads bent and close together as they talked, like they didn't want the others around them to hear whatever their conversation was. "I didn't know."

"I haven't talked to Demyan in … years. Well, since I moved back to Jersey, anyway."

"No better time," Ana said.

The moment Koldan caught sight of Ana, he stood from the bench. Demyan followed suit, offering his sister a small smile before it disappeared. It didn't matter how happy Demyan actually was in life, he rarely gave an ounce of the emotion away, especially when other people were around to see it.

Ana held her hand out for Koldan to take. He did, pressing a feather-light kiss to her knuckles in the process.

"This is a surprise," Koldan said, tugging Ana into his side.

"Sofia convinced Cora to take the boys so we could go out. I figured here was as good of a spot as ever," Ana explained.

Koldan nodded. "Sure. We're just … chatting."

"Right," Sofia drawled, gazing around at the amount of Bratva in the room. "What are you really doing?"

Demyan laughed. Ana watched as her brother leaned forward and pressed a chaste kiss to Sofia's cheek. The two had dated long ago, but as far as Ana knew, they'd ended that shortly before Demyan's wife came along. But, Sofia and Demyan had remained friends, even if it was at a distance.

Taking his spot back at Koldan's side, Demyan said, "Always the observant one, Sofia."

"Of course. How have you been, Demyan?"

"Wonderful," Ana's brother answered. "You?"

"Perfect," Sofia replied. "How's your wife?"

Demyan grinned. "Beautiful, as always."

"I'm happy to hear it. And the babies?" Sofia asked.

"Vera is our little ballet star and Roman is … a hellion."

Sofia winked. "Just like this father, then."

"So my father keeps saying." Glancing to the side, Demyan said, "And speaking of the hellion, here he is."

Ana tousled her nephew's hair as he flew past her, instantly seeking out his father. It wasn't uncommon for Demyan to let Roman tag along with him for business things, if that's what he was in Jersey for. Four-year-old Roman stood at his father's side with a toy car in one hand and a bottle of apple juice in the other.

"You brought your son to a club?" Sofia asked.

Demyan shrugged. "He wanted to come. I'm not drinking, I'm doing business. What's the problem?"

"Not a thing, I suppose."

Roman looked up at his father, grinning widely. "Guess what I did, Papa?"

"What, little man?" Demyan asked.

"I got away from Moore."

Demyan sighed, his gaze sweeping the crowd. "The whole point of Moore is that you don't get away from him, Roman."

"But this is *fun*, Papa," Roman said like it should have been obvious.

"Who?" Ana asked.

"Moore," Roman repeated, tipping his bottle up for another drink. "He's my cow."

"Bull," Demyan corrected.

"Cows are bulls."

"No, bulls are—"

"Boy cows with no milk," Roman interrupted. "That's what Ma says."

Demyan tried to hold back his smile and failed miserably. Ana couldn't help but laugh, as did Koldan and Sofia.

"Supposed to be his job, Papa," Roman said, tugging on his father's slacks.

"Watching you? Yes, I'm aware. It's what I pay him for, Rome."

"He's not very good at it."

"No, you're just very sneaky," Demyan grumbled under his breath. "Best fucking bodyguard in the family."

"And a four-year-old gets away from him," Koldan said, cocking a brow.

"Would you like to watch my son for a week?" Demyan asked. "He's like Houdini."

Koldan held his hands up, conceding. "Nah, I'll take your word for it."

"What's a Houdini?" Roman asked.

"A person not a thing," Ana said to her always curious nephew. "It's awfully late for you to be out, Roman. What did you bribe your papa with to get him to bring you?"

Roman grinned, flashing his white teeth.

Her nephew was too predictable. Roman had a way with his father, and Demyan didn't know how to deny the boy a thing.

Demyan shook his head at the sight of his son's knowing smirk.

"Nothing," Roman said.

"Liar," Demyan muttered. "He snuck into the car, and I was already backing out of the driveway when I noticed him."

"Seriously?" Koldan asked.

"As a fucking heart attack. I called Claire to let her know. The worst part? She wasn't even surprised."

"Bad words," Roman informed.

"I bought you a car on the way here. That's your hush money, kid. Anything else and you're going to have to owe me."

Roman nodded seriously. "I'll take it. Where's Moore? He's probably worried about me, Papa."

Demyan gave Koldan a look that Ana couldn't decipher. "We good, man?"

Koldan took the hand Demyan offered and shook it. "Perfect, man. Get your little trickster home."

"Will do." Demyan gave Ana a one armed hug. "I will see you at the end of the month for the supper at Ma's, yeah?"

"Sure," Ana said.

Demyan disappeared into the crowd of people in the VIP section. Roman was right under his father's feet the whole time.

"Christ, that kid is something else," Koldan said.

Ana agreed. "He's a lot like Demyan at that age. Or at least, that's what Ma and Papa say."

"How so?" Sofia asked.

"Articulate, above his age group, and intelligent."

Koldan smiled. "He's still just a kid under it all, though."

"He is." Ana crossed her arms, facing Koldan. "What's going on in here tonight, anyway?"

"Nothing, babe."

"Koldan."

Her husband sighed, rubbing at his forehead. "Demyan and I had a couple of guys try to work together on something. They fucked it up, of course, and somebody ended up with a bullet between his teeth." Koldan waved at the men drinking and talking in the VIP section before saying, "He brought some men and so did I. We were just …"

"Making nice for show," Sofia said, filling in the blanks.

"It looks good for you to show up, I suppose," Koldan said, grinning at Ana. "I wouldn't bring my wife into a gun fight, after all. You could have called me first, *krasivyy*."

"I didn't know you were handling Bratva business tonight," Ana said. "I thought you were just working."

Koldan cleared his throat and shoved his hands into his pockets. "I am working, babe."

Ana blinked, realizing that he was right. They weren't normal. Their life was never going to be normal. Koldan's work would never be normal.

"I'll call next time," Ana promised.

"Thanks."

"Shouldn't Dad have been here?" Sofia asked. "I mean if there was trouble between families or whatever?"

"No trouble," Koldan said, killing that idea before someone else could overhear. "Which was why Demyan came tonight, so we could stop that shit before anyone got crazy ideas. As far as Dad goes, he wasn't interested in showing face."

"He's the boss," Sofia said.

Koldan's expression didn't change as he replied, "Is he?"

What was that supposed to mean?

CHAPTER SIXTEEN

Ana barely managed not to trip over her sons as they scrambled into the kitchen ahead of her. Koldan turned from his spot at the stove in just enough time to catch both of his sons. At four and two respectively, their sons were loud as hell and always on the go of some sort. Ana usually thought it was funny because their father was so laid back and calm.

Tornadoes.

That's what her boys were. She loved them all the more for it.

"Slow down," Ana said, laughing.

"PAPA!" the boys shouted, trying to climb up Koldan's sides.

Like the patient man he was, Koldan gave his boys all the attention they wanted until they calmed down.

"Morning, *krasivyy*," Koldan said, kissing Ana's cheek as she came up beside him.

"Morning. Damn, you look good working at the stove."

Koldan grinned as he worked on his egg and bacon mess. "Wanted to do something for you this morning. Give you a break or whatever."

Giving the pan another look, Ana's stomach suddenly turned inside out. The smell of the food wafted upwards, and she barely managed to hold the vomit back. Taking a step away from the stove, Ana wondered what in the hell was up with her.

Koldan noticed instantly. "Hey, you okay?"

Ana shook her head, confused. "Yeah, sure. I'm just … not all that hungry, maybe."

He didn't look like he believed her for a second. "You love eggs, Ana."

She did.

And bacon.

But right then, she felt like she was two seconds away from vomiting all over the floor.

Her two boys clamored up to the kitchen table, demanding food. Ana's head spun.

"Ana?" Koldan asked, stepping into her line of vision again.

"Yeah?"

"You're turning white, *krasivyy*."

Was she?

"I'm going to go lie down," Ana said. "You okay with the boys?"

Koldan frowned but nodded. "Sure, babe."

Thankful for the weekend and the fact her boys had nothing scheduled to do for that Saturday and Sunday, Ana made her way back upstairs and to her bed. The second her head hit the pillow and she was wrapped up in the sheets that smelled like her and Koldan, Ana felt better. The nauseous sensation passed, and Ana drifted off to sleep.

Something warm and comforting woke Ana shortly after. She smiled at the sound of Koldan's humming as he kissed a path over her forehead, across her closed lids, and down to her lips.

"That's a good way to wake up," Ana said, her voice scratchy from sleep.

"Hey," Koldan murmured.

Ana opened her eyes to stare at her husband who was smiling. There was still a worried glint in his eye, though. "Hey."

"Boys are napping."

"Is it noon already?" Ana asked, confused.

"A little after one, actually. What happened this morning, *krasivyy*? You worried me."

"I'm sorry. I just didn't feel well."

Koldan sighed heavily, rolling his thumbs over her cheek bones. "All right. How're you feeling now?"

"Better," Ana whispered. "Much, much better if you keep touching me."

His grin was wicked. "I will, but I'd feel better if you got up and moved around a little first."

"I'm fine, Koldan."

"Just indulge me, Ana, please."

Not wanting to argue with her husband, Ana got out of the bed like he asked. Standing up made her realize how badly she needed to pee. Waving so he could see she was fine on her own two feet, Ana disappeared into the master bathroom and shut the door to do her business.

As she turned, something off to the side caught Ana's eye. Her birth control pills sat on the back of the sink, waiting for her to take her morning pill. She took it right after breakfast every morning. She'd used the shot for several years, but after her first son's birth, she'd switched to the pill for an easier transition of coming off a birth control method.

Checking over the pack, Ana noted she hadn't missed a pill, and she was already three days into her sugar pills that were supposed to be taken during her cycle. But last month …

Last month she'd gotten a minor infection in her ear after taking the boys swimming at an indoor pool. The drops hadn't worked all that well and the infection traveled into her throat. Her doctor prescribed an antibiotic.

It was a stupid mistake to make. The doctor had even warned her to use a backup method but it just slipped her mind. With her two boys and life and everything else …

"Oh," Ana said, louder than she must have realized.

"Ana?" Koldan asked outside the bathroom.

Ana was stunned.

Completely, utterly stunned.

"Ana," Koldan said again, firmer the second time. Ana turned and opened the door. "Are you okay?"

"Fine," Ana said, still unsure but smiling wide.

He would be so excited.

Koldan wanted another baby. He'd been bugging her about a third for the last year.

"I need you to go to the store," Ana said.

"Why?" Koldan asked.

"I think I might be pregnant."

Koldan froze. "Really?"

Ana nodded, biting her lip. "I think so."

She didn't get the chance to say another thing because Koldan stepped into the bathroom, grabbed her face in his hands, and pulled her in for a kiss that took away the air right from her chest. He held her close to his body and kissed her deeper until her fucking knees were weak, and she couldn't think.

Good *God.*

She loved this man.

"I love you, Ana," Koldan said, resting his forehead to hers.

Ana laughed, breathless and spun. "Go to the store."

"On it, babe."

CHAPTER SEVENTEEN

"So perfect," Koldan said, holding Sasha Viviana high in the air. The baby girl giggled down at her father, her little legs kicking in her footie pajamas. "And so pretty, my *dushka*. Giving your daddy heart attacks already, just thinking about beating the boys off."

Ana laughed from the couch. "You've got years before you have to worry about any of that."

Koldan eyed Ana from the side as he balanced Sasha on his hip. "That's not the way a father's mind works, Ana. We panic about it for years leading up to it."

"Hmm."

"What?" her husband asked.

"I wonder if that's how Anton felt for me."

Koldan shrugged. "I don't doubt it. Maybe I get why he hated me just … stealing you away like I did."

"You didn't steal me away," Ana said, scoffing.

"I kind of did."

Ana chose not to push her husband on the topic.

Koldan went back to giving little Sasha all of his attention. He was bound and determined to spoil that girl right rotten. Sasha didn't seem to mind. At only six-months-old, she was a daddy's girl through and through. Just getting Koldan in her line of sights, sent Sasha into a smiling fit of a creature. If Koldan didn't immediately pick her up, Sasha would scream loud enough to break the windows.

Sasha could do without Ana so long as Koldan was around. Their daughter was absolutely gorgeous. Big, wide blue eyes. Dark hair like Ana's with the ringlet curls to match. Her skin was creamy peach with a pretty pink tone around her cheeks. She had her mother's features and her father's color.

No doubt, the girl was going to be beautiful.

She already was.

Already, Sasha was trying to crawl, she'd spoken her first word—Papa, of course—and she had a little attitude that topped it all off. And Koldan didn't mind indulging that attitude every single chance he got, too.

Ana was maybe … finally … beginning to understand what her mother talked about for all those years when it came to Ana and her own father.

"You're spoiling her," Ana said.

Koldan grinned, tossing his daughter high again. "She's my pretty little princess, Ana."

Ana sighed.

"Of course, I'm going to spoil her," Koldan added. "No one, besides her mother, is as perfect as her. Leave me be, Ana. Let me spoil her."

"Fine," Ana whispered, still smiling.

"No more, though," Koldan said, giving Ana a look from the side.

"Huh?"

"Children. I think we've filled the house more than enough, don't you?"

Ana shrugged. "You didn't know it, but three was my limit, Koldan."

Koldan chuckled. "Mine, too. But after this little one …"

"She's perfect," Ana murmured.

"She is."

Ana listened for any noise coming from her sons' rooms upstairs. It was silent. She'd laid them down an hour before, but sometimes Adrik and Daniil would sneak out of their respective rooms and play in the hallway for an hour before Koldan had to go up and put them down for bed again.

"Boys are quiet," Ana noted.

Koldan smiled. "They are. I wonder what hell they got into that we didn't hear."

Koldan's statement was probably truer than either of them wanted to admit. Ana was still struggling in some ways to see her sons as the little Bratva princes that everyone else called them. They followed their father around constantly. Koldan didn't hide things from them. Lessons about family and loyalty and honor had become commonplace and Ana knew when Koldan talked about those things, it was more than just their family.

It was the Bratva family, too.

But she loved her boys. She loved them entirely, so she let them be. They would grow up to be whatever they wanted to be, and she could love them just the same as she did now.

"By the way," Koldan said, grinning as he avoided Sasha's bubbly, spit kisses.

"What's that?" Ana asked.

"I'm going to have your bulls sticking a little closer than normal, all right? They'll be visible, but they won't approach you unless something comes up and they need to."

"Why?"

Koldan shifted on his feet and sat Sasha to the carpeted floor. Instantly, the girl made grabby motions to her father to be picked back up again, but Koldan turned to Ana.

"What's going on, Koldan?" Ana asked.

"We just had a run in with a rival gang a couple of weeks ago. It's nothing too bad, but a couple of the crews retaliated. I just want to be safe, Ana, that's all."

Ana frowned. Koldan had taken his father's spot over the last couple of months. The transition had been easy for Koldan's men, as far as Ana understood, but it seemed like the issues outside of the Bratva piled on higher at the worst possible time.

"What about the boys? School and pre-school, Koldan."

"They have bulls that watch them, Ana."

"I know that, but they're not inside the schools, Koldan."

Koldan conceded to her point. "They're as close as they can be without breaking trespassing laws. The boys are in private, well-guarded schools. I'm more concerned about you. From now on, you need to be sure your bulls know where you're going every single time you make a step."

"Fine," Ana said quietly.

"I know you don't like this."

Ana smiled sadly. "I like that you take care of us."

Koldan chuckled deeply. "That I do."

"I'll take Sasha up to bed. Meet me in the bedroom in five?" Ana asked, winking.

"Absolutely."

Ana had just rounded the top of the stairs as the sound of glass breaking stopped her in her tracks. Fear crawled up her spine and lodged in her throat when she heard Koldan shout. Another loud bang followed, like someone was thrown against wood.

Or like someone had hit their front door.

Ana turned with her six-month-old baby girl in just enough time to see Koldan hit the bottom of the stairs. He didn't take his eyes off Ana's frozen form for a second.

"Safe room," he shouted.

Ana blinked, holding a crying Sasha tighter.

"Go, Ana!"

Koldan's hand hit Ana's back hard, lurching her forward. Rapid pops, one after the other, sounded downstairs. Her heart pounded out of control, threatening to leap right out of her chest. She hit the hallway running with Koldan right on her heels. Ana yanked open the doorway to Daniil's room just as Koldan turned the doorknob on Adrik's.

"Ma?" Ana heard little Daniil cry.

The noise downstairs got louder.

"Come here, baby," Ana whispered, trying to keep calm for her son.

What was happening downstairs?

Who would do that?

Ana grabbed Daniil's little hand in hers, trying to pretend like her own wasn't shaking. Koldan had a sleepy, confused Adrik in his arms as he jerked his head toward the back of the hallway. Ana followed his lead. Quickly, Ana found herself inside a room in their house she had never needed to use.

It was a small, eight by six box surrounded by ten inch thick steel. It had an air ventilation system and food stocked. It also had two little cots. Once closed completely, the door couldn't be reopened from the outside. A monitor was set up for the people inside the safe room so they could hear what was going on outside, and there were several camera shots showing the house on three separate screens.

Koldan sat Adrik to the floor and turned, hitting the red button on the wall.

Ana watched in silence and terror as the door to the room began to close and her husband didn't come inside. She held onto Sasha as the baby girl cried for her father. She didn't let go of little Daniil's hand when he reached out for Koldan, asking for him to stay.

"Koldan," Ana whispered.

Koldan touched two fingers to his lips and then turned away.

CHAPTER EIGHTEEN

Ana stayed still and quiet behind the steering wheel of her Benz as her mother helped Daniil and Adrik out of the backseat. Viviana unbuckled little Sasha from her car seat and cooed at the child.

"Ana?" Viviana asked softly.

"Yeah, Ma?"

"I'll take the kids in and get them something to eat. Sound good?"

"Sure. Thanks, Ma."

Ana said nothing when her father slid into the passenger seat. Anton waited until Viviana and the kids were inside the house before he turned to his daughter.

"Talk to me, *dushka*," Anton said.

Ana shuddered, her fingers clenching tight around the steering wheel until her knuckles turned white. "I just … had to leave. I can't even go inside my house because of the fucking cops. My kids were in that house. I *can't* …"

"You're okay," Anton said gently. "The boys and Sasha are fine. Koldan did well, Ana. He made sure you were protected and safe. What more could he have done?"

"Not brought it into my home at all!" Ana shouted.

Anton flinched. "Oh, my *dushka* … you just don't get it. Do you honestly believe that man wanted a bunch of gang members to storm your house and shoot it up? Do you truly think he would put you and his children in that position, Ana?"

"It happened," Ana argued. "If it wasn't for the goddamn men he had watching the house—"

"Ana, stop it."

Ana sucked in a deep breath, choking on a sob. "That was too real."

Anton frowned. "Ana, this life is not a game."

"I know that!"

"Then you know that Koldan did his best. He did everything he should have. And you cannot run away from your marriage and your choices every time something happens that you don't like, *dushka*. How is that love, Ana? How is that showing him that you understand and that you forgive his mistakes and accept him for who he is?"

Ana cringed. "I didn't run away."

"You did or you wouldn't be in Little Odessa right now," Anton argued.

"Stop it," Ana whispered, willing the tears away.

She couldn't stop the damned things. They were like a constant flood of her emotions and hurt streaking down her face. How she made the two and a half hour drive from Jersey to Brooklyn without crashing, Ana wasn't sure.

"I just need a couple of days," Ana said, hoping her heart would calm. "Just to think and get away from that so I can go back and not be angry with him."

Anton nodded. "Okay."

"Please don't be angry with me, Daddy."

"For what?" Anton asked. "Why on earth would I ever be angry with you, my *dushka*?"

"Because I'm not like Ma, and I can't always be okay."

Viviana Avdonin was the strongest woman Ana knew. Her mother had seen and experienced more things because of the mafia than some of the men who worked for Ana's father. Viviana rarely seemed to blink a lash at any of it. Ana tried to be that kind of person, the Bratva wife, unaffected.

But she couldn't always do that.

She'd failed.

People, angry with her husband, had come into their house and could have killed Ana and her children. How was she supposed to turn her cheek to that?

"Oh, Ana," Anton said, sighing heavily. "I'm not mad at you. You're not your mother. You don't have to be."

"Don't I?" Ana asked.

She was the wife of a Bratva boss, after all.

"No, because you're just perfect for him. Nobody else matters."

• • •

Ana stepped out of the car, hugging her middle as she glanced up at the man sitting on the front steps of the large home. Koldan rested his arms over his knees and watched her like he was waiting for her to bolt.

Ana's heart broke.

Maybe her father had been right.

Maybe she had run.

Ana let the boys out of their car and booster seat from the back of the Benz. Adrik and Daniil wasted no time getting out and running across the large driveway to their father's waiting arms. Koldan laughed as the boys climbed into his lap. Ana smiled as her husband kissed her boys' heads and hugged them tight.

The police tape was gone.

The broken windows were fixed.

The glass that had sprinkled the driveway and Koldan's shot up car had been removed.

It was like the ambush and attack hadn't even happened.

Not physically, anyway.

Ana could still feel the aftereffects lingering, especially in her heart.

She grabbed Sasha's car seat from the backseat, balanced the seat on her hip and crossed the driveway. Koldan stood to greet his wife, sadness playing in his gaze even though he smiled.

"*Krasivyy*," Koldan murmured. "The house doesn't feel right when the boys aren't tearing it apart."

Ana smiled. It was honest and true. She'd missed him over the last two weeks. Her unexpected trip to Brooklyn kept her there longer than she first meant to stay. "Oh?"

"No." Koldan took the car seat from Ana and set it to the step. Bending down, he playing with little Sasha's kicking feet. "Hello my princess. Papa missed you, baby girl."

Sasha cooed. "Pa, pa, pa."

Adrik and Daniil had already made their way into the house like nothing was amiss. They weren't frightened or worried. Ana wished she could say the same.

Standing straight, Koldan held out a hand for Ana. She took it without question. "And I missed you, Ana."

"Did you?"

"Yes," Koldan said. "So much."

"I'm sorry I took off."

Koldan shrugged. "I'm sorry you felt like you had to."

Ana let him tug her into his chest. She let herself be suffocated by that feeling of his warmth and love. It was a constant in their life. No matter what happened, that was always there. Koldan's lips brushed over Ana's cheekbone, seeking her mouth. She took his kiss, needing it.

Their life certainly wasn't perfect. Ana wasn't perfect.

"We're okay," Ana whispered.

Koldan nodded and held her tighter. "As long as you're here, everything is beautiful."

Because she was his.
"Always."

ABOUT THE AUTHOR

Bethany-Kris is a Canadian author, lover of much, and mother to three very young sons, one cat, and two dogs. A small town in Eastern Canada where she was born and raised is where she has always called home. With her boys under her feet, a snuggling cat, barking dogs, and a spouse calling over his shoulder, she is nearly always writing something ... when she can find the time.

Find her on Facebook at facebook.com/bethanykriswrites, on her website at www.bethanykris.com or Twitter - @BethanyKris.

Sign up to Bethany-Kris's New Release Newsletter at http://eepurl.com/bf9lzD to be notified when new releases are out.

ACKNOWLEDGMENTS

First and foremost, I want to thank the main hero of this series. The Avdonin family was just a silly dream of mine. A Russian man who talked to me like my characters do sometimes, and one day I decided to indulge his voice and put him on paper. He was my first mob boss, and while he wasn't as violent or as bloody as some of the ones I wrote after him, he was the first. And that made him so incredibly important to me. He shaped how I wrote heroes each time I sat down to pen a new man once I was done writing Anton's story. He continues to shape how I write them. And so, he deserves mentioning and gratitude, even if he is only fictional.

To my readers, the ones who have stuck through this series, the ones who begged for the story to continue, even when I said it wouldn't be pretty, thank you. I don't think you realize it, but you made this series worth it for me. You made it worth writing when it seemed more difficult than fun. You made it worth my time and effort. Your messages and time means the world to me. Thank you for loving this series, this fictional family of mine, as much as you have. In some ways, it was you who made this family more real to me.

To the girls who worked on this series with me in one way or another, editing, proofing and pre-reading, thank you. Tracy, Elle, and Eli. Words just aren't good enough. My biggest fans, always in my corner.

Jay Aheer … your work on the Guns covers have always been some of my favorites. Your talent is amazing, and you always hit on just what I'm looking for or needing. It's invaluable. You capture my words in a cover, and for that, I am forever grateful. Thank you.

I know I said once that Shattered was the end of *The Russian Guns*. In a way, it was. *The Jersey Vignettes* was simply my thank you to the readers, my gift for your enjoyment and love, while saying goodbye in my own way to the Avdonins.

And thank you.

—Kris

OTHER BOOKS IN THIS SERIES

The Russian Guns

The Arrangement, Book One
The Life, Book Two
The Score, Book Three
Demyan & Ana, Book Four
Shattered, Book Five

OTHER BOOKS BY THIS AUTHOR

Filthy Marcellos

Filthy Marcellos: Antony, Book 0.5
Filthy Marcellos: Lucian, Book One
Filthy Marcellos: Giovanni, Book Two
Filthy Marcellos: Dante, Book Three
Filthy Marcellos: Legacy, Book Four
Filthy Marcellos: The Complete Collection

The Chicago War

Deathless & Divided, Book One
Reckless & Ruined, Book Two
Scarless & Sacred, Book Three
Breathless & Bloodstained, Book Four

www.ingramcontent.com/pod-product-compliance
Lightning Source LLC
LaVergne TN
LVHW011047110826
845149LV00015B/3388

* 9 7 8 1 9 8 8 1 9 7 0 7 4 *